SADDLEBACK Classics

DRACULA

BRAM STOKER

ADAPTED BY

Emily Hutchinson

SADDLEBACK PUBLISHING, INC.

SADDLEBACK *Classics*

The Adventures of Tom Sawyer
Dr. Jekyll and Mr. Hyde
Dracula
Great Expectations
Jane Eyre
Moby Dick
Robinson Crusoe
The Time Machine

Development and Production: Laurel Associates, Inc.
Cover and Interior Art: Black Eagle Productions

SADDLEBACK PUBLISHING, INC.
3505 Cadillac Ave., Building F-9
Costa Mesa, CA 92626-1443

ISBN 1-56254-262-1

Printed in the United States of America
09 08 07 06 05 04   6 5 4 3 2 1

CONTENTS

1 Journey to Transylvania

Passages from Jonathan Harker's journal:

May 3. So far, my business trip to Eastern Europe has taken me through London, Munich, Vienna, and Budapest. While in London, I visited the library at the British Museum. I found out that Count Dracula lives in the Carpathian Mountains. This is one of the wildest and least known areas of Europe. I read that every known superstition in the world comes from Transylvania — my final destination. If so, my stay there should be very interesting.

It was evening when we got to Bistritz. Count Dracula had directed me to go to the Golden Krone Hotel. I was greeted by a cheerful, elderly woman who gave me a letter from the Count. In it, he said that his carriage would meet me at the Borgo Pass tomorrow and bring me the rest of the way.

I asked the hotel manager if he knew anything about Count Dracula or his castle. At the mention of Dracula's name, both he and his wife crossed themselves. They insisted that they knew nothing at all of the man and refused to speak further.

May 4. Just before I left the hotel, the old lady came to my room. "Must you go?" she asked worriedly. "Do you know what day it is? It is the eve of St. George's Day. Tonight, when the clock strikes 12, all the evil things in the world will come out."

Then she got down on her knees and begged me not to go. "At least," she said, "wait one or two days." It all seemed very ridiculous, and I did not feel comfortable.

There was business to be done, however. I could let nothing get in the way of it. My employer, Mr. Hawkins, had sent me to deliver some papers to Count Dracula. They were the ownership documents for the London estate he had bought.

I told the old lady I must go. Worriedly, she then took a crucifix from around her neck and put it around mine. "For your mother's sake," she said, and left the room.

May 5. The Castle. Yesterday, the trip from the hotel to the castle was quite frightening. When the other coach travelers heard where I was going, they looked at me with pity. Of course they did not speak English. Looking up some of their strange words in my dictionary, I found that they meant "werewolf" or "vampire."

It was after dark when we got near the Borgo Pass. Then suddenly, a horsedrawn carriage drew up beside the coach. The horses were splendid, coal-black animals. They were driven by a tall man wearing a great black hat. His face was hidden. I could only see the gleam of his eyes, which seemed strangely red in the lamplight.

I got out of the coach and into the carriage. Without a word, the driver shook the reins, the horses turned, and we swept into the darkness of the Pass. As I looked back, I saw the passengers in the coach crossing themselves. I felt a strange chill, and a lonely feeling came over me.

It seemed that we rode for hours. At a

few minutes before midnight, I struck a
match and looked at my watch. It was then
that I heard a wild howling. It seemed to
come from all over the countryside. The
horses began to strain, but when the driver
spoke to them quietly they calmed down.
Then the driver jumped to the ground and
disappeared into the darkness. A while later,
the moon broke through the clouds. I saw
around us a ring of wolves, with white teeth
and lolling red tongues.

Then I saw the driver standing in the
roadway. He swept his long arms about, as
though brushing something away. As if at
his signal, the wolves fell back! Just then a
heavy cloud passed over the moon again,
and we were in darkness.

A feeling of dread came over me. I was
afraid to speak or move. The driver got back
into the carriage, and we went on. It seemed
like a very long time before we pulled into
the courtyard of an old castle.

The driver jumped down and helped me
out of the carriage. He placed my bags on
the ground beside me. Then he jumped again

into his seat, shook the reins, and drove off.

I stood in silence at the door, for I did not know what to do. There was no bell or knocker. What sort of place had I come to? My business trip was becoming a nightmare.

Just then, I heard a heavy step behind the great door, and a key was turned. When the door opened, a tall old man looked out at me. He was clean shaven except for a long white mustache. He was dressed in black from head to foot. He held an antique silver lamp. The old man motioned me in. "Welcome to my house!" he said. "Enter freely and of your own will!"

As soon as I was inside, he shook my hand. His fingers were cold as ice! His hand was like that of a dead man.

"Count Dracula?" I said uncertainly.

He bowed and replied, "I am Dracula, and I bid you welcome, Mr. Harker. Come in. You must need food and rest." He carried my bags along a hall, up a winding staircase, and down another hall. At last he threw open a heavy door. Inside I saw a well-lit room in which a table was spread for supper. A

fire was burning in the fireplace. He showed me another room right off this one. It was a welcome sight, for it was a large bedroom with another bright log fire.

"I pray you, sir, be seated and have something to eat. I won't be eating with you, as I have dined already," said my host.

After I had finished eating, we spent some time talking. I could not help but notice that his appearance was very unusual. His ears were pale and extremely pointed at the top. His chin was broad and strong, and the cheeks were firm but unusually thin.

His hands were rather coarse. Strange to say, there were hairs in the center of his palms. The nails were long and fine, and cut to a sharp point. As the Count leaned close, a horrible feeling of nausea came over me. Somehow the Count must have noticed my discomfort, for he drew back.

As I looked toward the window, I saw the first dim light of the coming dawn. The Count quickly rose and said, "But you must be tired. Your bedroom has been made ready for you. Tomorrow, you shall sleep as late as you want. I must be away until the afternoon, so sleep soundly and dream well!"

2 The Mysterious Castle

Passages from Jonathan Harker's journal:

May 7. It is again early morning. I have rested and enjoyed the last 24 hours. Today I found breakfast waiting for me. A note from Dracula was beside my plate. In it he explained that he had to be away for a while. After breakfast, I opened a side door in the dining room and found a sort of library.

In the library I discovered shelves of English books, magazines, and newspapers. While I was looking at them, the door opened, and the Count entered. He told me that he had been studying English ever since he had thought of going to London. Then he said that he wanted me to stay for a month to help him with his English. His plan was to speak it well enough so that he would not be seen as a foreigner when he moved to London. I did not want to stay that long, but

Mr. Hawkins had told me to assist Count Dracula in any way I could.

Dracula then wanted to know about the house that Mr. Hawkins had arranged for him to buy. He asked me all about the neighborhood and the estate. When I told him all the details, he said, "I am glad the house is old and big. I myself am from an old family. To live in a new house would kill me. I am glad to hear there is an old chapel there, too. We Transylvanian nobles do not like to think that our bones may be among the common dead."

We talked late into the night and fell asleep in our chairs. At dawn, the crow of a rooster startled us awake. Count Dracula jumped to his feet. In great haste he said, "Why, here it is morning again! I am sorry to have kept you up so late, Mr. Harker." With a bow, he left me.

May 8. There is something so strange about this place that I cannot help but feel uneasy. I am beginning to wish that I had never come. I fear I must be the only living soul in the entire castle!

Today I set up my mirror by the window and was just beginning to shave. Suddenly I felt a hand on my shoulder and heard the Count saying, "Good morning." I jumped, for it amazed me that I had not seen him in the mirror. In jumping, I had cut myself slightly, although I did not notice it at the moment. Answering the Count's greeting, I turned to the glass again to see how I had been mistaken. This time there could be no error. The Count was right behind me, and I could see him over my shoulder. *But I could not see him in the mirror!*

Just then, I noticed the cut because it had begun to bleed a little. The blood was trickling over my chin. Without warning, the Count suddenly made a grab at my throat! As I drew back, his hand touched the string of beads that held the crucifix around my neck. It made an instant change in him.

"Take care how you cut yourself," he said. "It is more dangerous than you think in this country." Then he grabbed my mirror. "This is a foul sign of man's vanity," he said. "Away with it!" He opened the window and threw out the mirror. In the courtyard far below, I heard it break into a thousand pieces. Then he left without a word.

When I went into the dining room, breakfast was waiting as usual, but the Count was nowhere to be seen. I ate alone. How odd that I had not seen Count Dracula eat or drink. What a very strange man he must be!

After breakfast, I explored the castle. There were doors everywhere—but all of them were locked and bolted. There was no place to get out except from the windows in the castle walls! And the castle is on the edge of a cliff. A stone falling from any of the windows would drop a thousand feet without touching anything.

I have seen the Count making my bed and setting the table in the dining room. Now I wondered—if he himself does all these chores, there must be no one else to do them. This thought gave me a fright. If there is no one else in the castle, it must have been the Count himself who drove the coach that brought me here. If so, what does it mean that he could control the wolves, as he did, by simply holding up his hand? Why did all the people on the coach fear for my visit here? Bless that good, good woman who gave me the crucifix!

May 12. Tonight the Count came to my room. He told me he would be away for the evening. Then he said, "Let me warn you of something, my friend. Do not go to sleep in any other part of the castle. If you get drowsy in another room, return to your own bedroom right away. You will then be safe."

A little while after he left me, I went up the stone stair to look out toward the south. It gave me a feeling of freedom to look out. As I leaned from the window, my eye was caught by something moving below me. It was near the windows where I imagined the Count's rooms were. What I saw was the Count's upper body coming out from the window. I did not see his face, but I knew him by his neck and hands.

I was at first surprised and somewhat amused. But then I saw him pull the rest of his body out the window and crawl down the castle wall! He was *face down,* his cloak spreading out around him like great wings! At first I could not believe my eyes, but I kept looking. I saw his fingers and toes grasp the corners of the old stones. He continued to move downward—much like a lizard moves down a wall.

What kind of creature is he? The dread of this horrible place suddenly overpowered me. It seems there is no escape for me. The castle is a prison, and I am a prisoner here!

May 15. Tonight I saw the Count go out in his lizard fashion. I decided to make use of this time by exploring the castle. But every door I tried was locked. At last, however, I found an open door. Inside was a room full of old, comfortable furniture. There I sat at a little oak table and gradually felt a sense of peace come over me.

May 16. Am I mad? Let me be calm. The Count's warning frightened me a bit at the time. Yet when I think of it now, it frightens me even more. Last night, while I sat at the oak table writing in my journal, I began to feel sleepy. So I put my journal back into

my pocket. I remembered the Count's warning, but I took pleasure in disobeying it. I must have fallen asleep there—but now I wonder.

I was not alone. In the moonlight across from me were three young women. Was I dreaming? Although the moonlight was behind them, they cast no shadow on the floor. One was fair and the others were dark. The women came close to me and looked at me for a long time. Then they whispered together and laughed. All three had brilliant white teeth that shone like pearls against their red lips. One said, "Go on! You are first, and we shall follow."

Another woman added, "He is young and strong. There are kisses for us all." The fair girl came forward and bent over me. Her breath was sweet, but there was a bitter smell under the sweetness—the odor one smells in blood. She licked her teeth and lips. I could feel her hot breath on my neck.

Suddenly the Count appeared. Throwing down a bag he was carrying, his strong hand grasped the woman's slender neck. His eyes were blazing bright red as he pulled her back. Then, with a sweep of his arm, he threw the woman from him, and motioned to the others. It was exactly the same gesture the carriage driver had used to drive off the wolves!

"How dare you touch him, any of you? How dare you even look at him when I had forbidden it? *Get back*, I tell you! This man belongs to me! I promise you that when I am done with him, you shall kiss him at your will. Now go!"

"Are we to have nothing tonight?" said one of them. She pointed to the bag that he had thrown upon the floor. It moved as if there were some living thing in it. When he nodded his head, one of the women jumped forward and opened it. I heard a gasp and a low wail, like that of a half-smothered child. The women then disappeared from the room with the dreadful bag.

Yet how did they leave the room? There was no door near them. *They seemed to have faded into the rays of the moonlight and passed out through the window!* As horror overcame me, I sank down unconscious.

The next morning I awoke in my own bed. The Count must have carried me here.

A Grim Discovery

3

Passages from Jonathan Harker's journal:

May 18. This morning I went down to look at that room again. Now I felt that I *must* uncover the truth. Was I dreaming, or did it really happen? But the door is now locked.

June 25. It has always been at night when I have felt I was in danger. I have not yet seen the Count in the daylight. Does he sleep when others wake, so he may be awake while they sleep? If I could only get into his room! But there is no possible way. The door is always locked.

Yes, there might be a way—if one dares to take it. Where his body has gone, why may not another body go? I have seen him crawl from his window. Why should I not do the same, and go in by his window? I shall risk it. The worst that can happen is death. A man's death is not like a calf's.

Heaven may still be open to me. God help me in my task!

Some days later. I have made the effort, and, with heaven's blessing, have come safely back to this room. Last night I went straight to the window on the south side. The stones were big and rough. The mortar between them had been worn away. By going slowly, I was able to make my way to the Count's window. Soon I was standing on the windowsill, opening the window.

I slid through the window feet first. The room was empty! It was barely furnished and littered with odd things that seemed never to have been used. Everything in it was covered with dust.

At one corner of the room was a heavy door. I found that it led through a stone passage to a circular stairway. The steps were steep. At the bottom was a dark, tunnel-like passage. As I went through the passage, I noticed a bad smell that grew closer and stronger as I walked along. At last I opened a heavy door that stood ajar. I found myself in an old chapel that had evidently been used as a burial place. Inside the chapel were 50 boxes shaped like coffins. Each one was filled with freshly dug earth. In one of the boxes, stretched out on a pile of earth, lay the Count!

He was either dead or asleep. I could not say which. His eyes were open and stony, and his lips were as red as ever. But there was no sign of life—no pulse, no breath, no beating of the heart! I fled from the place and left the Count's room by the window. Crawling up the castle wall, I finally reached my own room. Exhausted, I threw myself on the bed and tried to think.

June 29. I was awakened by the Count. He told me that I would be going home tomorrow. I do not trust him. I am not sure what he is planning, but I do not believe he will let me go home.

After he left my room, I thought I heard a whispering at my door. I softly crept to the door and listened. It was the Count's voice, saying, "Back, back, to your own place! Your time has not yet come. Wait. Have patience. Tomorrow night, tomorrow night, is yours!" There was a low, sweet ripple of laughter. In a rage I threw open the door. The Count was gone, but the three terrible women were standing there, licking their lips. As I stared at them, they all joined in a horrible laugh. Then they turned and ran away.

June 30, morning. With the dawn, I knew that I was safe. I was determined to get out of the castle today. Knowing that the front door would be locked as always, I decided to find the key. Now I knew where to find the monster who kept the key.

The earth-filled box was in the same place. I knew I must search the body for the key. As I looked at the Count, I saw something that filled my soul with horror. Now he looked much younger. The white hair and mustache had become a dark iron-gray. His cheeks were fuller. His mouth was redder than ever. On his lips were trickles of fresh blood.

I had to search him, or I was lost. I shuddered as I bent to my task. But try as I might, I could not find the key. Then I stopped and looked at the Count's face. His lips seemed twisted in a mocking smile.

The truth came over me. This was the being I was helping to transfer to London! There, perhaps for centuries to come, he would satisfy his thirst for blood. Perhaps he would continue to create a new and ever-widening circle of demons to help him. The very thought drove me mad. A frantic desire came upon me to rid the world of this monster. I seized a shovel and aimed it at his head. But as I did so, his eyes turned and gazed at me, full of hate. His evil glare seemed to paralyze me, and I dropped the shovel and ran.

In a growing panic, I made my way back to my room. I must get away from this dreadful place! Tonight I shall climb down the castle wall to the courtyard. And then away for home! If I don't make it, then goodbye, my dearest Mina!

4 Mina Visits Whitby

Passages from Mina Murray's journal:

July 24. Lucy met me at the station, looking sweeter and lovelier than ever. We went directly to the Crescent Inn, a lovely place. Between the inn and the town is an old church with a big graveyard full of tombstones. Strangely, I think this is the nicest place in Whitby. It has a full view of the harbor and the bay—where the headland stretches out into the sea. There are pleasant walking paths lined with benches all through the churchyard. All day long people sit here looking at the beautiful view and enjoying the breeze.

This will be a lovely vacation with Lucy and her mother. I am worried about Jonathan, though. He left England many weeks ago. At first he wrote to me every day, about his trip and about Transylvania. Then, suddenly, his letters stopped. I hope and pray he's not in any danger.

July 25. Lucy and I sat in the churchyard for a while today, enjoying the view. She told me all over again about Arthur and their coming marriage. That made me just a little heartsick, for I haven't heard from Jonathan in more than two months. I wonder where he is and if he is thinking of me! With all my heart I wish he were here right now.

July 26. It is so helpful for me to express my worries in this journal. It is like whispering to myself and listening at the same time. I am concerned about both Lucy and Jonathan. Although she seems well, Lucy has lately taken to her old habit of walking in her sleep. Her mother has spoken to me about it. We have decided that I am to lock the door of our room every night.

Mrs. Westenra has read that sleepwalkers may sometimes go out on roofs of houses and along the edges of cliffs. If they are suddenly awakened, they are said to fall over with a despairing cry. Poor dear! She is naturally worried about Lucy. She tells me that her husband, Lucy's father, had the same habit.

Lucy is to be married in autumn, and she is already planning how her house will be arranged. I enjoy doing the same thing. Jonathan and I, however, will begin our married life in a very simple way. We shall have to try hard to make ends meet.

Lucy's fiancé, Arthur Holmwood, is coming here for a visit. I think Lucy is counting the minutes until he arrives. She wants to take him up to our favorite bench on the churchyard cliff. There is no better place to show him the beauty of Whitby!

July 27. No news from Jonathan. I am getting quite uneasy. I *do* wish he would write, if only a single line. Lucy has been sleepwalking more than ever. Each night I am awakened by her moving about the room.

August 3. Another week gone, and no news from Jonathan. Oh, I do hope he is not ill! Lucy is still walking in her sleep. She tries the door, and finding it locked, goes about the room looking for the key.

August 6. Another three days, and no

news. If I only knew what was happening, I would feel better. Last night the weather was threatening. The fishermen say we are in for a storm. Huge gray clouds are piling up like giant rocks. The fishing boats are racing for home. They rise and dip in the high waves as they sweep into the harbor.

August 7. Whitby has just experienced one of the greatest storms in its history! It started a little after midnight. First there was a strange sound from over the sea. Then the storm broke. Wild winds turned the sea into a roaring monster. Soon the giant waves broke over the piers and swept over the lighthouses. Then thick fog came drifting in, so damp and cold that it seemed almost eerie. At times we could glimpse the sea churning in the glare of the lightning. Loud thunder seemed to make the sky tremble.

One ship had a lot of trouble getting in. Many of us watched its struggle from the beach. Finally, leaping from wave to wave, the ship entered the harbor and was pitched up on the beach. The searchlight guiding it in revealed a horrible sight. Tied to the helm

was a corpse! No other form could be seen on deck. A great awe came over all of us who were watching on the beach. As if by a miracle, the ship had found the harbor — steered by the hand of a dead man!

As soon as the ship touched shore, a big dog jumped up on deck from below. It leaped from the bow onto the sand. Then it ran for the cliff that lies below the church graveyard and disappeared.

Later it was found that the dead man at the helm was holding tightly to a crucifix.

A bottle containing a little roll of paper was found in his pocket. The paper proved to be part of the ship's log. A doctor said that the man must have been dead for two days.

August 9. The tale told in the ship's log was startling. It turned out that the boat had come from Russia. Its only cargo was a number of large wooden boxes filled with dirt. This cargo was addressed to a lawyer named Thomas Snelling who has offices here in Whitby. The dog that jumped off the ship seems to have disappeared entirely. No doubt the poor thing was frightened and is hiding somewhere in terror.

Early this morning, a big dog belonging to a local coal merchant was found dead. The poor animal must have been in a fight. Its throat was torn away, and its belly was slit open as if by a savage claw.

The ship's log told a terrible story. The crew had reported to the captain that a strange man was on board. Oddly, the stowaway was seen only at night. Since the ship had booked no passengers, this was a great mystery. Then members of the crew started disappearing one by one. They always disappeared at night, while on watch. Soon only the captain was left.

August 11, 3:00 A.M. I can't sleep now, so I may as well write. Last night, I fell asleep easily. Then in the middle of the night, I suddenly woke up, with a horrible sense of fear upon me. Lucy was gone. The door was shut, but not locked, as I had left it. I threw on some clothes and went to look for her. She was nowhere in the house. I ran outside and looked toward our favorite bench in the churchyard. The silver light of the moon struck a half-reclining figure on the bench. Something tall and dark bent over the snowy white figure.

I ran toward the churchyard as fast as I could. As I got closer, I called "Lucy! Lucy!" The dark figure raised its head. From where I was, I could see its white face and red, gleaming eyes. Lucy did not answer, and I ran closer. Then a cloud blocked the light of the moon for a minute or so. When the cloud passed, I could see Lucy's head tipped back on the back of the bench. She was quite alone.

There was no sign of any living thing about.

She seemed to be asleep. But as I came nearer to her, she pulled the collar of her nightdress close around her throat. She shuddered, as if feeling cold. I put my shawl around her and fastened it at her throat with a big pin. Then I woke her up and helped her back to the house.

Safe in her bed, Lucy quickly went back to sleep, after asking me not to tell her mother about her sleepwalking. Knowing the poor state of her mother's health, I agreed.

August 11, noon. Lucy is still asleep. I was sorry to notice that I must have been clumsy when pinning the shawl last night. The skin of her throat is pierced in two places. When I apologized, she said she did not even feel it. Luckily, it will not leave a scar, as the marks are so tiny.

August 12. Lucy tried to sleepwalk twice last night. I am glad I remembered to lock the door. I still haven't heard from Jonathan. What can be wrong?

August 14. After dinner, Lucy had a headache and went to bed early. I went out for a walk along the cliffs. As I arrived back home, I looked up at our window. I saw Lucy's head leaning out, and I waved to her. She did not notice me. Just then, the moonlight fell on her, and I could see that Lucy's head was on the windowsill and her eyes shut. Next to her, seated on the windowsill, was something that looked like a big bird. Thinking she might get a chill, I hurried upstairs. She said she was just sleepwalking back to bed. But I noticed that she was holding her hand to her throat, as if to protect it from cold.

August 15. Lucy seems very tired. She slept late again today. And Mrs. Westenra gave me the bad news that her own health is getting worse. Dr. Seward says that she has heart problems.

August 17. Still no news from Jonathan. Lucy seems to be getting weaker, and so does her mother. I do not understand why Lucy is so frail. She eats well, sleeps well, and enjoys the fresh air. Yet the color in her cheeks is fading. I looked at her throat just now as she lay asleep. The tiny wounds from the pin seem not to have healed. If anything, they are larger than before. I think I should have Dr. Seward look at them.

August 19. Joy, joy, joy! But not all joy. At last, news of Jonathan. The dear fellow has been ill. That is why he did not write. For six weeks he has been in a hospital in Budapest, suffering from a brain fever. The nun who wrote me the letter said that he has been delirious. He has been talking about wolves and poison and blood—and of ghosts and demons! I will leave Whitby in the morning and go to nurse him. Then I will bring him home.

August 24. The trip to Budapest was tiring, but I didn't care—for I would be with Jonathan at last! When I finally got to him, I found him pale and weak-looking. He is a wreck of himself. He says he does not remember anything of the past few months. I know he wants me to believe this, so I won't ask any questions. But he has had some terrible shock—that is easy to see.

We decided to be married right away, and we were—right in the hospital! Jonathan sat up in bed, propped up with pillows. He answered his "I will" firmly and strongly. I could hardly speak, I was so happy. I am Jonathan's wife at last, Mina Harker!

As soon as Jonathan is better, we will go back to Whitby. Lucy and Arthur are planning to be married on September 28. I am sure we will be there by then.

5 Lucy's Strange Illness

Passages from Dr. Seward's journal:

September 2. I have been called in to look at Lucy Westenra. Her condition is not good. For some reason she seems to have lost a lot of blood. I tested her blood, and it is normal. Still, she complains that it is hard to breathe at times. She says she has dreams that frighten her, but she can remember nothing about them. I can find no cause for her illness. That's why I have sent for my old friend, Professor Van Helsing of Amsterdam. He knows a great deal about rare diseases.

September 7. Van Helsing examined Lucy today. I myself was shocked at how much she has worsened in just one day. She is very pale. The red is gone from even her lips and gums. The bones of her face stand out. Her breathing is painful to see or hear. The Professor said that she needs a blood transfusion right away, or she will die.

Lucy's fiancé, Arthur, came over just as I was getting ready to give my blood. He insisted on being the one to do it. As the transfusion went on, a flush of life seemed to come back to poor Lucy's cheeks. When it was over, I could see that Arthur was weakened. Van Helsing told him to go home and rest. "You have saved her life this time," said Van Helsing. "You have done all that you can for now."

After Arthur left, the Professor adjusted Lucy's pillow. As he did so, the black velvet band that she wore around her neck was pulled up a little. We saw a red mark on her throat. There were two small wounds just over the jugular vein. I saw no sign of disease, but the edges of the wound were white and worn-looking. How could these small pinpricks have caused her to lose so much blood? To make her so pale, the whole bed should have been covered with blood!

Van Helsing said that I must sit up all night with Lucy. "See that nothing disturbs her. You must not sleep all the night," he warned me. He himself had to go back to Amsterdam for more books and supplies. It was a struggle, but I did stay awake all night. Lucy slept peacefully. In the morning, she seemed better. The maid took over her care, and I went home to get some sleep.

September 8, evening. When I returned to check on Lucy, she was in good spirits. Arthur had had to leave town for a while to take care of his sick father. He promised that he'd be back as soon as possible.

Lucy and I spent a charming evening together. I was glad to see how improved she was. After supper, she showed me a room next to her own. "No sitting up tonight for you!" she said. "You are worn out, and I am quite well again. You can sleep in the next room. I shall leave your door open and my door, too. If I want anything, I promise to call out, and you can come to me at once." I was too tired to argue.

September 9. I woke up when I felt Van Helsing's hand on my head. "How is our patient?" he asked.

"She was quite well when I left her—or

rather when she left me," I explained.

"Come, let us see," he said. Together, we went into the room.

A deadly fear shot through my heart as I looked upon the girl. She was horribly white and more weak-looking than ever. Even her lips were white, and her gums seemed to have shrunken back from her teeth! The Professor felt her heart, and after a few moments, he said, "It is not too late. Her heart beats, though weakly. But all our efforts are undone. We must begin again. Young Arthur is not here now. I'm afraid I will have to call on you this time, John," he said to me.

He got out his instruments for the transfusion, and I rolled up my sleeve. We began immediately. I must say that I had a feeling of pride as I saw the color come back into her pale cheeks and lips. Afterward I felt faint and a little sick. But after a short rest and some breakfast, I felt much better.

Lucy slept most of the day. When she woke she was better and stronger. Van Helsing stayed with her during the night, and I went home to rest.

§ 6 A Garlic Wreath

Passages from Dr. Seward's journal:

September 10. This afternoon I went back over to see how Lucy was doing. While I was there, a large package came for Van Helsing. He opened it and showed us a great bundle of carefully wrapped white flowers. "These are for you, Miss Lucy," he said. "They are medicines. This is how they work: I put some in your window, and I make a pretty wreath to hang around your neck."

Lucy smelled the flowers and wrinkled her nose. Pushing them away, she said, "Why, these flowers are nothing but common garlic!"

"I warn you that you *must* do this," the Professor said. "If not for your own sake, then for the sake of others." Then he and I decorated the entire room with the flowers. He rubbed them all over the windows and

windowsills, on the doorframe, and around the fireplace. He then made a wreath and placed it around Lucy's neck. Before we left, he said to her, "Do not remove this wreath. And even if the room gets hot, do not open the window or the door tonight."

After Lucy promised to follow his instructions, Van Helsing and I left. We needed a good night's rest, for we were both very tired. Van Helsing seemed very sure that Lucy would be fine in the morning, but I felt a vague sense of terror.

September 11. Van Helsing and I went to see Lucy at 8:00 in the morning. Mrs. Westenra greeted us and said that Lucy was much better. Then she told us that she had looked in on her daughter last night and found the room very warm. She was surprised to find a lot of strong-smelling flowers everywhere. Mrs. Westenra had removed them all before opening the window.

The Professor was very upset at this. When we looked in on Lucy, we found her worse than ever. She needed another blood transfusion. This time Van Helsing would have to provide the blood. Once again, we watched as the color slowly returned to Lucy's cheeks.

Van Helsing then spoke very firmly to Mrs. Westenra. He said that she must not remove anything from Lucy's room without asking him first. The flowers were part of the cure, he explained.

September 17. For the past several days the Professor and I have taken turns watching over Lucy. Fresh garlic arrives from Amsterdam every day. Now it looks as if she will be all right. We will leave her in her mother's care tonight.

September 18. We never should have left Lucy—even for one night. When we arrived today, we found Lucy's mother dead and Lucy barely breathing! The wounds in her throat looked horribly white and mangled. A window had been broken. There was evidence that a huge animal, possibly a wolf, had been in the room. The fright must have been too much for Lucy's mother—her weak heart had given out. Trying to defend her daughter from the animal, Mrs. Westenra had apparently grabbed the wreath of garlic from Lucy's neck.

Now Lucy seemed to lie near death. We did everything we could for her, even giving her another blood transfusion. But nothing helped. She kept getting weaker. Her pale gums were drawn back from her teeth—which unexplainably looked longer and sharper than usual. In the afternoon, she asked for Arthur, so we sent for him.

When Arthur arrived at about 6:00 in the evening, Lucy seemed to gain a little strength.

September 20. We are all exhausted from watching at Lucy's bedside. Her breathing is very difficult, and her face looks terrible. Perhaps it is because her mouth is open and her gums are so pale. Perhaps it is some trick of the light, but Van Helsing agrees that her canine teeth look longer and sharper than the rest.

Earlier tonight, I heard a sound at the window. In the light of the full moon, I could see a great bat outside. When I came back to my chair, I found that Lucy had moved slightly. Soon after, she awoke, and I offered her some food. She did not seem interested in it. In fact, she did not even seem to be interested in going on with the struggle for life and strength.

At 6:00, Van Helsing examined Lucy's throat. "My God!" he exclaimed. I bent over and looked, too. As if by magic, the wounds on her throat had completely disappeared!

The Professor said, "She is fading away. It will not be long now."

Van Helsing was right. Shortly before she died, Lucy asked Arthur to kiss her. She spoke in a strange, deep voice that I had never heard before. When Arthur bent over her, Van Helsing grabbed him and dragged him back with more strength than I knew he possessed. He hurled the young man across the room.

"Not for your life!" he said. "Not for your living soul and hers!" Then he stood between them as if holding a lion at bay.

I kept my eyes on Lucy, and saw a look of rage come over her face. The sharp teeth clamped together. Then her eyes closed, and she started to breathe heavily.

Soon after that, she opened her eyes again and looked at the Professor. "My true friend, and his!" she said. "Oh, guard him well, and give me peace!"

"I swear it!" Van Helsing promised, kneeling beside her. Then he told Arthur to kiss Lucy on the forehead, once. Within minutes, the poor girl was dead. I led Arthur to the next room, where he sat down, covered his face with his hands, and sobbed.

Back in the room, I found Van Helsing staring at poor Lucy. His face was sterner than ever. Some change had come over her body. She now looked very calm and peaceful. "Unfortunate creature!" I said. "It is the end of her suffering at last."

He turned to me and said, "Not so, alas! It is only the beginning!"

I asked him what he meant. He only said, "We can do nothing yet. Wait and see."

The funerals of Lucy and her mother were arranged for a few days later. After the undertaker had done his work, Van Helsing and I took one last look at the pretty young woman. In death, all of her loveliness had returned. I found it hard to believe that I was looking at a corpse!

September 25. It has been three days since Lucy and her mother were put into the tomb. In those three days, several strange cases have been reported. It seems that some young children returned home late after playing on the heath. When they finally did get home, they reported that they had been with a "bloofer lady." What this means, no one knows.

The odd thing is that some of the children

have been slightly wounded in the throat. The wounds look as if they could have been made by a rat or a small dog. The police are keeping a sharp lookout for lost children — especially those who have been near the heath. They are also looking for any stray dogs that may be about.

7 The Count Returns

September 22. So much has happened since my last entry! Jonathan has recovered very nicely, and we are back in London for the time being. Today we went for a walk, and were enjoying ourselves very much. At one point I was looking at a very beautiful girl, in a big hat. She was sitting in a carriage outside Giuliano's. Suddenly, Jonathan clutched my arm so tight that he hurt me. Under his breath he said, "My God!" When I turned to him, his eyes seemed to be bulging out in terror and amazement.

He was gazing at a tall, thin man, with a narrow nose, a black mustache, and a pointed beard. The man was also looking at the pretty girl. In fact he was looking at her so hard that he did not see either of us, so I could study him closely. His face was hard and cruel. His big white teeth were pointed like an animal's. His lips were very red. "It is the man himself!" Jonathan said.

Jonathan was clearly terrified about something. He kept staring. A clerk came out of the shop with a small package and gave it to the lady in the carriage. As the carriage drove off, the dark man kept his eyes fixed on her. Then he hailed a cab and followed her.

"It is the Count, but he has somehow grown young!" cried Jonathan. "Oh, my God! If I only knew! If I only knew!" He was so upset that I was afraid to ask him any questions. Remaining silent, I led him to a park bench under a shady tree. After a moment of stunned silence, Jonathan suddenly fell asleep with his head resting on my shoulder.

In about 20 minutes, he woke up. "Why, Mina, have I been asleep?" he asked quite cheerfully. "Oh, do forgive me. Come, dear, and we'll have a cup of tea." He seemed to have forgotten all about the stranger.

Jonathan's illness must have affected his memory. I am now determined that I must somehow learn the facts of his journey.

Later that day. This afternoon I received a telegram from a Professor Van Helsing—whoever he may be. It said, "You will be grieved to hear that Mrs. Westenra died five days ago, and that Lucy died the day before yesterday. They were both buried today."

Oh, such sorrow in just a few words! Poor Mrs. Westenra! Poor Lucy! Gone, gone, never to return to us. And poor, poor Arthur, to have lost such sweetness out of his life!

September 23. Jonathan is better after a bad night. He will be at work all day. While he is gone, I will read the journal he kept while he was away. Perhaps I shouldn't—but I *must* know what happened to him.

September 24. Poor Jonathan! How he has suffered, whether in fact or only in his imagination! I wonder if there is any truth in his story. And yet he seemed so certain of that man we saw yesterday.

Another letter from Van Helsing arrived

today. He says he needs to talk to me about Lucy. I immediately sent him a telegram saying he should take the next train.

September 25. Van Helsing has come and gone. Oh, what a peculiar meeting! I feel like one in a dream. If I had not read Jonathan's journal first, I should never have believed what Van Helsing said. But now I know that every horror Jonathan described in his journal is true.

September 26. Last night at dinner, I told Jonathan that I had read his journal. I also told him about Van Helsing's visit and what he had said about Lucy. Jonathan seemed relieved to hear all of this. Now that he *knew* his suspicions were true, he felt better. He said that he was no longer afraid—not even of the Count. Jonathan also said that he thinks Van Helsing is just the man to hunt out the monster Transylvanian.

8 Van Helsing's Plan

Passages from Dr. Seward's journal:

September 26. Van Helsing returned from London yesterday after visiting Mina Harker. When he got back, he showed me a London newspaper. He pointed to a story about children being lured away from their play. "What do you think of that?" he asked. One paragraph described the small puncture wounds found on the children's throats.

As I read, I immediately suspected that these wounds were caused by the same beast that injured Lucy. Van Helsing explained that I was wrong. He told me that it was far worse than that. He claimed that the wounds had been made by Lucy herself! Of course, I did not believe him.

Van Helsing insists on proving it to me tonight. He says we have to go to the churchyard where Lucy is buried—a strange request! Yet I have told him I will go with him. In truth I have no idea what he plans to do.

September 27. Last night, I accompanied Van Helsing to the churchyard. He had the key to the Westenra tomb. As he opened the creaky door, he motioned me to go inside. Following me in, he lit a candle. Then he approached Lucy's coffin and took some tools from his bag.

"What are you going to do?" I asked.

"Open the coffin. It's the only way I can convince you that what I said is true."

As soon as he got the coffin open, I looked inside. It was empty.

This was certainly a surprise—no, a *shock*—to me. "Do you believe me now, John?" Van Helsing asked calmly.

"The fact that Lucy's body is not here does not prove that she injured those children," I said. "Perhaps the body was taken by body-snatchers." I knew that sounded foolish, but it was the only explanation I could think of. Van Helsing sighed and shook his head.

"Well," he said, "I see you need more proof. Come with me."

He put the lid back on the coffin, gathered up his tools, and blew out the candle. We left the tomb. Then he told me to keep watch at one side of the churchyard while he watched at the other.

It was midnight when we began our watch. At around 2:00 A.M., I thought I saw something like a white streak. It was moving toward Lucy's tomb. Out of the darkness, the Professor hurried toward me. He was leading a small child who was saying something about the "bloofer lady."

"Is the boy wounded?" I asked.

"We shall see," said Van Helsing. We examined the child's throat. It was without a scratch or mark of any kind. "It seems that we were just in time," said the Professor. We took the child home and then went home ourselves.

Van Helsing has promised to come at noon tomorrow. We will go back to the tomb in the daytime.

September 28. Lucy's body is back in her coffin today. She seems more beautiful than ever! It is hard to believe that she has been dead for over a week. Van Helsing says that

Lucy is neither dead nor alive, but *undead*. To save her and others, he says that we must drive a stake through her heart. Then we must cut off her head and stuff her mouth with garlic. We plan to come back tonight, with Arthur.

September 29. Last night we waited by Lucy's tomb. Near dawn she returned to it, bringing another child with her! Her mouth was covered with blood, and the child was crying. She threw him down to the ground before returning to her coffin. Arthur and I stared in shock. It was proof enough that Van Helsing was telling the truth about her!

Van Helsing said that he was willing to perform the operation that would save Lucy's soul. But then he had a second thought. Perhaps the task should go to the one who had loved her best. After it was done, Lucy's soul would be free to join the angels. And the children she had wounded would return to normal. Arthur said that he would be the one to restore Lucy to us as a holy—rather than an unholy—memory.

As Arthur drove the stake through Lucy's heart, the thing in the coffin screeched. The body shook and twisted wildly. Its sharp white teeth champed together until its lips were cut. But Arthur did not stop until he was finished. When it was over, a calm came over the body. Once again, it looked like the Lucy we had all loved. After sending Arthur out of the tomb, we sawed the top off the stake, leaving the point of it in the body. After that, we cut off the head and filled the mouth with garlic. We then closed the coffin and hurried out of the wretched place.

Outside the air was sweet, the birds sang, and there was peace everywhere.

Van Helsing said that we still had work to do. We had to find Dracula and stamp him out. This would be very difficult, but it had to be done. We promised to stick together until the bitter end. We agreed to meet in two nights.

When I returned home, there was a telegram from Mina Harker. It said that she and Jonathan are coming to Whitby for a visit. I look forward to their arrival tomorrow.

September 30. It was such a pleasure to meet Jonathan Harker! But what a shock to hear that Count Dracula's property in England is right next to mine! The name of the estate is Carfax. Knowing where he lives, it may be easier than I thought to find his hiding place. Then our goal is to discover where he keeps the dirt-filled boxes he had shipped from Transylvania.

I am afraid it won't be so easy to rid the world of the evil Dracula. Van Helsing has told me that this vampire is stronger than 20 men. He can, within some limits, appear at will— whenever and wherever he wishes! And he can appear in several different forms. He can direct storms, fog, and thunder. He can command the rat, the owl, the bat, the moth, the fox, and the wolf. He can become larger or smaller. He can at times disappear.

How then are we to destroy him? It will be no easy task. Of that I am sure. But if we fail, *he* must surely win—and then where shall it end? To fail is not merely a matter of life and death. It is a matter of saving our very souls. For if he wins over us, we shall become like him—foul things of the night. The gates of heaven would be forever shut to us. No matter what, we must face this duty, to save ourselves and the world.

We are not without our own strength, of course. We have the resources of science. We are free to act and think. And the hours of the day and the night are ours equally. We are devoted to this cause, and we shall act together. I am confident we will win.

Van Helsing and I know some of his weaknesses. He cannot move around during daylight hours. He cannot enter a house for the first time unless someone who lives there invites him in. We know that the crucifix has power over him, as does garlic. There are other things, too. A branch of wild rose on his coffin will keep him trapped inside. A sacred bullet fired into the coffin will kill him. And he cannot cross running water. Only a stake through the heart — and the removal of his head — will give him rest.

First we must find his coffin. But we know he has *fifty* coffins, and we are not sure where they are! Tomorrow we will begin looking for them at Carfax.

9 Dracula Visits Mina

Passages from Dr. Seward's journal:

October 1. We didn't want Mina to have any part of this terrible plan. We left her at the hotel room so she could get a restful night's sleep while we—that is, Jonathan, Professor Van Helsing, and I—went to Carfax. We had to see how many of the Count's coffins were here in Whitby. The house itself was full of dust. We could tell where the Count had been walking, for the dust was disturbed in some places. The smell in the house was disgusting. It seemed as if every corrupt breath exhaled by that monster still hung in the air.

We found the coffins, but there were only 29 of them. The monster must have had the other coffins shipped elsewhere. Our job will be more difficult than we had thought. How will we find all the others?

October 2. The events of these past few weeks must have been very hard on young Mina Harker. Jonathan tells me that she slept quite late. He had to call two or three times before she awoke. Yet even then, she seemed to want to go on sleeping.

We think we may be able to trace the rest of the coffins. Perhaps Thomas Snelling, the lawyer who picked them up after the shipwreck, will know something.

October 2. We got in touch with Snelling and found out about the boxes. He gave us the addresses of the places to which they had been delivered. It seemed that they were all over London. They had been delivered in groups of at least six to a number of empty, old houses. When I visited these places, I found out that all of them had recently been sold. I didn't have to check with any lawyers to know who had bought them. Money had never been a problem for Count Dracula.

I had no doubt that the Count meant to distribute the boxes even further at some later time. Perhaps he planned to have each of the 50 coffins at a different location, eventually.

We will break into Carfax again and try to find the Count's keys. We can't be breaking into all the other houses in the heart of London! There are far too many people around who would see us. Somehow we will need to find keys to get into the other houses in town.

October 3. It occurred to me today that Mina Harker's need for so much sleep is not normal. Why didn't I think of it before? I suspect the Count. Has he been visiting her while we were away looking for the coffins? Tonight, I asked Van Helsing to come with me to the Harkers' room. When they did not answer the door, we broke it in.

What we saw sent a chill down my spine. On the bed beside the window lay Jonathan Harker. His face was flushed, and he seemed to be in a stupor. His wife was kneeling on the edge of the bed. Facing her stood a tall, thin man, dressed in black. When he turned, we could see that it was the Count. He was trying to force her face to his chest, and she was resisting with all her strength. Her white nightgown was smeared with blood,

and a thin stream of blood trickled down Dracula's chest.

As we burst into the room, the Count stared at us boldly. His eyes flamed with evil passion and his sharp, white teeth glistened like those of a wild beast. He threw Mina back upon the bed and moved toward us. But by this time, the Professor was holding up the crucifix. The Count suddenly stopped and backed up. He backed up farther as we advanced with the crucifix. Then a cloud crossed the moon and the room suddenly went dark. When we could see again, the Count was gone.

Mrs. Harker began screaming loudly. Her face was deathly pale, and her eyes were mad with terror. It took Jonathan a few minutes to awaken from the stupor. He seemed dazed for a few seconds, but then he came to himself.

"What does this mean?" he cried out. "Dr. Seward, Professor Van Helsing, what has happened? What is wrong? Mina, dear, what is it? How did this blood get here? My God! Has it come to this? Dr. Seward, do something to save Mina. It cannot have gone too far yet. Guard her while I look for him!"

Mina cried out. "No, no! Jonathan, you must not leave me. Stay with me!"

Van Helsing and I tried to calm them both. We asked Mina to tell us everything that had happened.

She told us that the Count had drunk some blood from her neck. He had said, "It is not the first time, or the second, that your veins have refreshed me." Then he forced her to drink some blood from a vein in his chest. If she refused, the Count threatened to kill Jonathan right in front of her. "From now on, Mina, you shall come to my call," the Count had said to her. "When my brain says 'Come!' to your brain, you shall cross land or sea to do so."

We could see two small wounds in her neck. Because she had resisted, I knew that she was not as yet completely under the Count's spell. She could still be saved, if we acted fast. As soon as the sun came up, we left, knowing that Mina would be safe during the day. Our plan was to spend the day destroying all of Dracula's dirt-filled coffins. At least, we could ruin them for Dracula's purposes. By placing a Holy Wafer in each coffin, we would purify the dirt so he could not use it.

The first place we visited was Carfax. There we purified the dirt in all of the 29 coffins. As luck would have it, we found a large key ring at Carfax. Now we would not have to break into the London houses, but could quietly open each front door.

That afternoon we took the train to

London. We would visit each of the other houses where we knew he had sent coffins. By evening, we should be finished. Then Mina would be safe.

October 3, later. We went to each house, purifying the dirt in each coffin. When we were finished, we realized that we had found just 49 of the 50 coffins. *Where could the last one be?* Until we had purified *all* the coffins, no one would be safe.

10 Mina Is Hypnotized

Passages from Jonathan Harker's journal:

October 4. We could not leave Mina alone during the night. Who could know what Count Dracula was planning to do? Whatever it was, we had to stay with her to protect her. So after we had purified all the coffins we could find, we quickly returned to Mina.

In the middle of the night, Mina sent me to get Professor Van Helsing. In two or three minutes, Van Helsing was in the room.

"I want you to hypnotize me!" she said. "Do it quickly—before the sun comes up. I believe that the Count has been getting into my mind. That is how he controls his victims. If his mind is so connected to mine, perhaps I can discover the Count's plan. Hurry, for the time is short!"

Professor Van Helsing did as she asked.

When her eyes took on a faraway look, he asked, "Where are you now?" Mina did not answer. He waited, and then asked again.

This time she answered him. "I do not know. Everything here is strange to me! I can see nothing. It is all dark."

"What do you hear?" asked the Professor.

"The lapping of water. Yes! And I can hear little waves rising and falling."

"Then you are on a ship?"

"Oh, yes!"

"What else do you hear?"

"The sound of men running about. Oh, yes! There is the creaking of a chain, and some loud, clanking noises."

By this time the sun had risen, and the windows revealed the full light of day. Professor Van Helsing snapped his fingers to wake her.

We knew that the Count could do nothing during the day. It was a comfort to know that the sun had just come up, and the whole day was ours. We decided to eat breakfast before doing anything.

After we ate, Mina asked, "Why must

we follow him? When he is leaving us?"

For a minute, Professor Van Helsing looked at her sadly. Then he said, "Just know this, my dear, dear Madam Mina— *now more than ever* we must find him."

"But why?" asked Mina.

"Because he can live for centuries—and you are but a mortal woman. Ever since he put that mark upon your throat, time is on his side, not yours!"

I was just in time to catch her as she fell forward in a faint.

The rest of the day, I stayed with Mina. Professor Van Helsing and Dr. Seward had gone off to the Port of London. We were sure that the Count must be on his way back home. The only thing we needed to know was which ship was taking him there.

October 5. Professor Van Helsing and Dr. Seward brought news from the port. For some reason, they asked Mina to leave the room while we talked.

They said they had spoken to some of the dock workers who remembered the Count. He was very strong, they said, and he had brought with him a big box on a cart. After taking the box off the cart himself, it took several men to lift it onto the ship, the *Czarina Catherine*. There could be no doubt that this was Count Dracula. By the time the Doctor and the Professor got wind of this information, the Count was well on his way to the Black Sea. From there he would no doubt continue up the Danube River toward his home in Transylvania.

Our plan is to take a land route, which is faster than traveling by sea. We will meet the ship when it gets to the mouth of the Danube River. Our best hope is to find him when he is in the box, during the day. Then it will be easier to deal with him as we must.

October 5, later. It is now clear why Mina was asked to leave the room. The Professor and the Doctor both see that Mina is becoming more and more like a vampire. I cannot see it—but perhaps that is because I am so close to her. Her teeth appear sharper, they say, and her eyes seem harder.

They also told me their thoughts about the state of her mind. When hypnotized, it seems that she can tell what the Count can see and hear. Surely, then, he can read *her* thoughts, too! That's why they believe that it is necessary for us to keep our plan from Mina. If she doesn't know it, she cannot give it away in her thoughts.

It is painful to think of keeping secrets from my beloved Mina. But it is for her sake that we must.

We know that the *Czarina Catherine* will take three weeks to reach the mouth of the Danube River. By traveling over land, we can get there in three days. Allowing for delays on our part and fast winds for the ship, we think we still have a margin of two weeks. We have decided to leave on October 17 at the latest.

October 6. Today Mina surprised us by saying that she wanted to go with us on our journey. She said that she would feel safer with us than if she were left behind. If the Count called to her through her mind, she would have to go to him, no matter what stood in her way. She would feel better if we could watch her at all times.

October 11. We have spent the past few days planning our trip. Now that I have made a will, all preparations seem to be complete. Mina, if she survives, will be my sole heir. If not, the others who have been so good to us shall have everything.

October 16. We left London yesterday, arrived in Paris last night, and took the Orient Express to Varna. Here we will wait until the *Czarina Catherine* comes into port.

Mina is well, although she sleeps a great deal. For about a half hour—right around sunrise and sunset—she is her old self again. At these times, there seems to be no outside force trying to control her. Van Helsing hypnotizes her at such times. While in a trance, she says that she hears waves lapping against the ship, and the sound of water rushing by. She can even hear the wind in the sails. But since she can see only darkness, we know that the Count is staying in his dirt-filled box while on the ship.

We know that Count Dracula cannot cross running water of his own will. That means that he cannot leave the ship even if he takes the form of a bat. If we can only get on board after sunrise, he will be at our mercy. Then we can open the coffin and put an end to him—as we did poor Lucy—before the evil monster wakes.

We told the shipper that the box contains something stolen from a friend of ours. That is how we got a paper telling the Captain to let us on board to inspect the box.

Arrangements have been made for a special messenger. He will tell us the instant the *Czarina Catherine* is sighted.

October 24. We have been waiting more than a week. While hypnotized each morning and evening, Mina speaks to us in a trance. She always gives us the same information: lapping waves, rushing water, and creaking masts. *Where is the ship?*

11 The Vampire Destroyed

Passages from Dr. Seward's journal:

October 28. Today we received word that the *Czarina Catherine* had docked at Galatz. How can this be? Galatz is an inland city on the Danube River. Why did the ship change its course?

Professor Van Helsing was the one who figured it out. He looked at Mina and said, "The Count has used your mind. He sent his spirit to you to find out where we were. Then he used all his powers to send the ship to Galatz. Now he is thinking of nothing but escape. At all costs, we must hurry. We must catch him before he gets back to his castle in Transylvania."

October 30, Galatz. Because the trains do not run often, it took us three days to get here. We went directly to the *Czarina Catherine*. At the docks we found out that a man named Skinsky had already picked up the Count's box! We tried to find Skinsky, but his landlord said he had not seen him for a few days. While we were talking to the landlord, a man came running up to us. He gasped that Skinsky's body had just been found—his throat torn open as if by some wild animal! We knew better.

October 30, evening. The Count's only goal is to get back to his castle. What choices were open to him? We knew that he must be brought back by someone. If it were otherwise, he would travel either as a wolf, a bat, or in some other way. No doubt he cannot cover such a distance during one night—so he must stay in his wooden box during the day.

The box must be taken by road, by rail, or by water. These are his only choices. If he is taken by road, there is too much chance of being discovered. Guards at every border would be sure to ask questions. If the box were opened during the day, one ray of the sun would be the end of him.

He cannot risk being taken by rail, either.

In a freight car, no one is in charge of the box. The train might be delayed, and any delay could be fatal, with his enemies—us— so closely on his trail.

The Count's only other choice is to go by water. But that, too, is dangerous, since he cannot travel over running water on his own will. If the ship were wrecked, he would die as soon as he hit the water. Perhaps he could cause a storm and have the vessel driven into land, as he did at Whitby. But once on land, what would he do without his many boxes full of dirt? At Whitby, at least, he had them with him. Still, traveling by water seems to be his best choice.

We looked at a map and figured out which river he would probably take. But there was no point in trying to follow him up the river. We knew that at some point he would have to travel by land. He had to travel over the Borgo Pass to get to his castle. So we will wait for him at the Pass.

November 3. We arrived at Borgo Pass just after sunrise. Mina and Van Helsing went on ahead to the castle, where we would meet them later. Jonathan and I did not want Mina to see what we had to do to the Count. In case our first plan failed, we made another. Van Helsing would purify any of Dracula's coffins that might still be stored at the castle.

Jonathan had reminded us of the three female vampires who lived there. Van Helsing was to find them and destroy them while they slept in their coffins. It was not at all like murder. Once their bodies were destroyed, the women's souls could find eternal rest.

November 6. For three days, we waited at the Borgo Pass. Finally, on the afternoon of the third day, a wagon drove by. There were two men sitting in front. The driver was urging the horses to go faster, but we could see that the wagon was carrying a heavy box. It looked exactly like the other 49 that we had purified in London! The driver did not stop for us, so we were forced to chase the wagon all the way to the castle.

Once we got to the castle, Van Helsing, Jonathan, and I had a fierce knife fight with

the driver and the other man. After many blows were struck, we won out. Jonathan had never been so strong as he was right then. With a mighty shove, he pushed the box to the ground. Then, with his knife, he pried off the cover. There lay the Count.

The fall from the wagon had scattered some dirt over him. His face was as white as death, and his stony eyes were burning with the terrible fires of hate. As we looked down at him, he looked up at the sky. But by now, the sun was beginning to set, and his look of hate was turning to one of victory. At that very moment, however, Jonathan stabbed the vampire in the throat and I plunged my knife into his heart.

It was like a miracle. Before our eyes, Count Dracula's entire body turned to dust and passed from our sight.

For as long as I live I shall be glad for one thing: On Dracula's face, in his last moment, there appeared a look of peace. It was the last thing I would have ever expected to see.

Afterword

Passage from Jonathan Harker's journal:

It has been seven years since we all went through the flames. Our happiness since then has been well worth the pain we went through. And now there is an added joy for Mina and me. Our boy's birthday falls on the same day she was saved from Count Dracula's spell!

Dr. Seward is now happily married. Our friend Professor Van Helsing acts as a kindly grandfather to our son.

With our boy on his knee, Van Helsing summed it all up in these words:

"This boy already knows his mother's sweet and loving care. Someday he will know what a brave and strong woman she is. He will then understand how some men loved her enough to dare much for her sake."